porcupette
finds a family

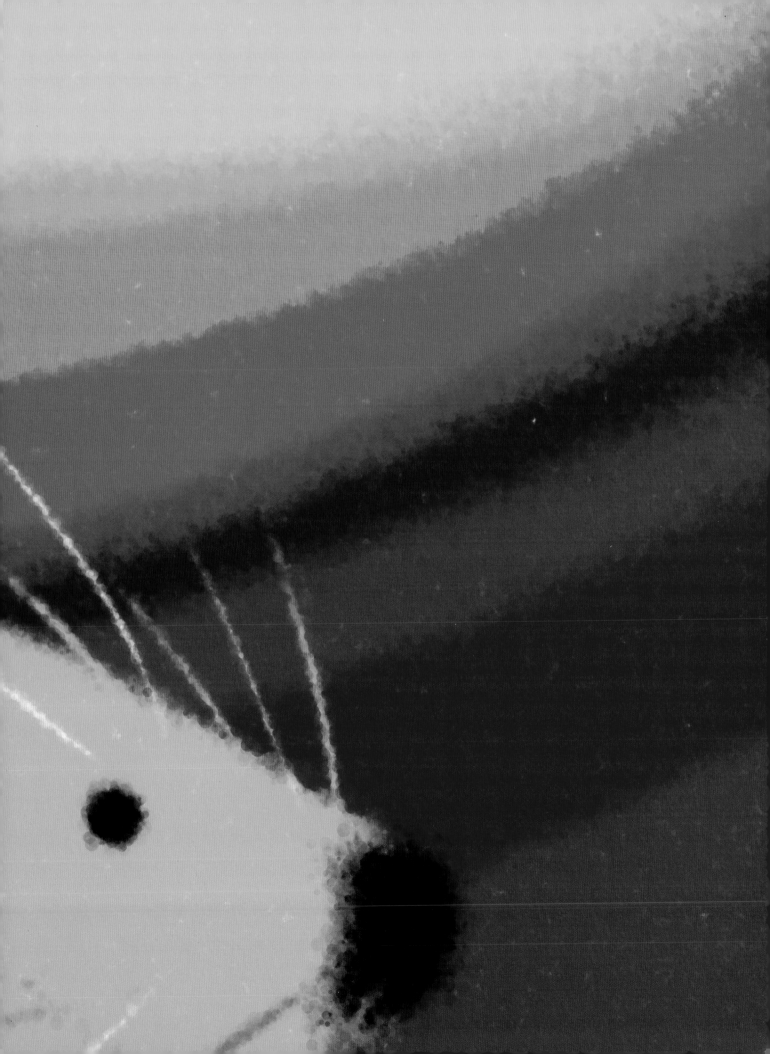

Vanita's Dedication

To all brave children who have to move on to another family
and to the parents who love them,
and, as always, to all my grandchildren.

Acknowledgements

Mike Blanc
Vince DeGeorge
Ben Kempf (porcupine expert)
Ellen Kempf
Paul Royer
Sheila Tarr
Kristin Blackwood
Kurt Landefeld
Michael Olin-Hitt
Jennie Levy Smith
Elaine Mesek

Text by Vanita Oelschlager
Illustrations by Mike Blanc

Printed in China.
Hardcover Edition ISBN 978-0-9819714-7-6
Paperback Edition ISBN 978-0-9819714-8-3

www.VanitaBooks.com

porcupette
finds a family

written by **vanita oelschlager**

illustrations by mike blanc

VanitaBooks, LLC

I am Porcupette. I am a baby porcupine. Baby porcupines are called "porcupettes."

I was born in Western Pennsylvania under a roof made of rocks.

I was born in the fall. Porcupines have quills to keep them safe. Quills are like small sharp stinging spears. My quills were soft at birth, but an hour after I was born, my quills got stiff. So, already I could hurt anyone who would try to hurt me.

My mother loved me very much. And I love her.
Every day she let me drink milk from her so I would grow
up healthy and strong. Then she would go out to find
food for herself.

She would tell me to stay under the rocks until she came back. When she did, she would take me on walks and show me berries and other things I would soon learn to eat.

I was happy and I knew I was loved until one day my
mother left me safe at home and went on her daily hunt
for food. She had always come back before. But this day
she didn't come back. I waited. I waited all night. I waited,
and still no mother. I tried not to be scared. But I was.

I peeked outside. I was afraid; so, I put my quills out to protect myself, like my mother had taught me.

I went out into the snow to find Mom.
I looked everywhere. I was really tired and really
hungry when I came to a cave. I peeked inside.

There was a mother bear and two babies. Baby bears are called "cubs." They were drinking milk from her. Mother Bear was sleeping.

I watched for a minute. I was not sure Mother Bear and her babies would want a prickly porcupine in their home. But I was so hungry and so tired and so sad that I did something that might have made my mother mad.

I walked into their cave and snuggled next to the
cubs and started drinking milk from Mother Bear. The
cubs were so hungry I think they hardly even saw me.
I was glad there was enough milk for them and me too.

I decided that until I found my mother, I would
pretend I was one of Mother Bear's babies. Maybe they
wouldn't notice I was different. Maybe Mother Bear
wouldn't see that I really wasn't her baby. I would only
play this game until my mother came back for me.

Soon the babies could see me. They thought I was a bear.

Mother Bear woke up and snuggled me just like her two cubs. They didn't seem to notice my quills. I wasn't so afraid so I kept them smoothed down.

Each day when we walked with Mother Bear I would
look for my mother. No luck. I began to miss her more
and more and more.

I began to think that maybe she left me for something I did wrong. Or maybe she left me because of something she saw that was unlovable about me.

What if Mother Bear leaves me too? Then I will be
all alone in the big wide world.

I tried not to think about Mother Bear leaving me,
but I was afraid they would notice I was not like them. I
was afraid they would not love me. I was afraid they would
not want me around. And you know what I do when I'm
afraid. I stick out my quills.

I started doing mean things to my brother and sister
bears. Sometimes I would stick them with my quills.
They didn't do anything to hurt me. Maybe I was afraid
they would.

They would cry out for Mother Bear. She would come and pick the quills out and lick their sore noses or feet. I knew Mother Bear knew what I had done. So surely she would leave me now.

But each night she would hug all three of us babies until we went to sleep. Maybe she really did love me. But my own mother left me. I was afraid Mother Bear would too. And do you know what fear made me do? I'd poke and stick my mom and family with my quills. I couldn't seem to stop doing things so that she wouldn't love me.

The cubs got very big, but I stayed small. They were soft and cuddly, but I was prickly. When would she stop loving me and go away, or take her real babies and leave?

Well, one day it happened. I was drinking my milk
with the others when I decided to use my quills on
Mother Bear. She growled and knocked us all off. She
started picking the quills out of her own nose.

The two cubs were mad at me and chased me up a tree. They wouldn't let me down. Each time I tried to come down they would growl at me and swat at me. But they kept away from my quills.

But even though she was mad at me, Mother Bear
called us all to come home, and the cubs ran off. I came
down. I was tired. I was mad at everyone. I said to myself,
"See? Nobody loves me."

I didn't go back to Mother Bear. I went off to find my old home under the rock. Well, I found it and I curled up. I just stayed there feeling sorry for myself.

I fell asleep, finally. What woke me up was a paw
reaching under the rock and pulling me out. I was scared.
I stuck out my quills. I made all the scary noises I had in
me. Soon I realized it was Mother Bear.

She picked me up with her mouth, quills and all.
She marched me back to the cave.

We all drank milk. Mother Bear pulled the quills out
of her mouth and paws. She held me until I went to sleep.

Do you know what? She did love me after all. She came looking for me. She was letting me be her baby. I wasn't afraid any more. My quills went down. My brother and my sister crawled in with me. I was happy for the first time since my mother went away.

I realized that if I just stopped being afraid, I would stop hurting my new family. I could be loved. I would take a chance that this mother wouldn't go away. I would let this mother love me.

And best of all, I would love them all back.

the author and artist

Vanita Oelschlager is a wife, mother, grandmother, philanthropist, former teacher, current caregiver, author and poet. A graduate of Mount Union College in Alliance, Ohio, she now serves as a Trustee of her alma mater and as Writer in Residence for the Literacy Program at The University of Akron. Vanita and her husband Jim were honored with a *Lifetime Achievement Award* from the National Multiple Sclerosis Society in 2006. She was the Congressional *Angels in Adoption* award recipient for the State of Ohio in 2007 and was named *National Volunteer of the Year* by the MS Society in 2008. Vanita was also honored in 2009 as the *Woman Philanthropist of the Year* by the Summit County Chapter of the United Way.

Mike Blanc is a life-long professional artist. His work has illuminated countless publications for both corporate and public interests worldwide. Accomplished in traditional drawing and painting techniques, he now works almost exclusively in digital medium. His first book *Francesca*, was written by Vanita Oelschlager and published in 2008. Other titles include *Postcards from a War*, and *Bonyo Bonyo, The True Story of a Brave Boy from Kenya* with co-illustrator Kristin Blackwood.

Mike's illustrations for this story were produced with Corel® Painter™ digital painting software for artists.

net profits

All net profits from this book will be donated to The Oak Adoptive Health Center at Akron Children's Hospital in Akron, Ohio.

The Center works to prepare and educate parents and families involved in domestic, international and special needs adoption. It also provides medical history evaluations, and psychological and developmental evaluations and support to encourage the healthy growth of the adoptive family.